This igloo book belongs to:

....

igloobooks

Illustrated by Natalie Hinrichsen

Copyright © 2017 Igloo Books Ltd

An imprint of Igloo Books Group,
part of Bonnier Books UK
bonnierbooks.co.uk.

Published in 2019
by Igloo Books Ltd, Cottage Farm
Sywell, NN6 0BJ
All rights reserved, including the right of reproduction
in whole or in part in any form.

Manufactured in China. GOL002 0519
10 9 8 7 6 5 4 3 2 1

Library of Congress Cataloging-in-Publication
Data is available upon request.

ISBN 978-1-83852-543-9
IglooBooks.com
bonnierbooks.co.uk

old MacDonald had a Farm

igloobooks

Old MacDonald had a farm, E-I-E-I-O,
and on that farm he had some hens, E-I-E-I-O.

With a cluck-cluck here and a cluck-cluck there,
here a cluck, there a cluck, everywhere a cluck-cluck.
Old MacDonald had a farm, E-I-E-I-O.

Old MacDonald had a farm, E-I-E-I-O,
and on that farm he had some chicks, E-I-E-I-O.

With a cheep-cheep here and a cheep-cheep there,
here a cheep, there a cheep, everywhere a cheep-cheep.
Old MacDonald had a farm, E-I-E-I-O.

Old MacDonald had a farm, E-I-E-I-O,
and on that farm he had some cows, E-I-E-I-O.

With a moo-moo here and a moo-moo there,
here a moo, there a moo, everywhere a moo-moo.
Old MacDonald had a farm, E-I-E-I-O.

Old MacDonald had a farm, E-I-E-I-O,
and on that farm he had a horse, E-I-E-I-O.

With a neigh-neigh here and a neigh-neigh there,
here a neigh, there a neigh, everywhere a neigh-neigh.
Old MacDonald had a farm, E-I-E-I-O.

Old MacDonald had a farm, E-I-E-I-O,
and on that farm he had some pigs, E-I-E-I-O.

With an oink-oink here and an oink-oink there,
here an oink, there an oink, everywhere an oink-oink.
Old MacDonald had a farm, E-I-E-I-O.

Old MacDonald had a farm, E-I-E-I-O,
and on that farm he had some ducks, E-I-E-I-O.

With a quack-quack here and a quack-quack there,
here a quack, there a quack, everywhere a quack-quack.
Old MacDonald had a farm, E-I-E-I-O.

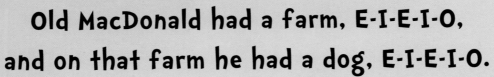

Old MacDonald had a farm, E-I-E-I-O,
and on that farm he had a dog, E-I-E-I-O.

With a woof-woof here and a woof-woof there,
here a woof, there a woof, everywhere a woof-woof.
Old MacDonald had a farm, E-I-E-I-O.

Old MacDonald had a farm, E-I-E-I-O,
and on that farm he had some sheep, E-I-E-I-O.

With a baa-baa here and a baa-baa there,
here a baa, there a baa, everywhere a baa-baa.
Old MacDonald had a farm, E-I-E-I-O.

Old MacDonald had a farm, E-I-E-I-O,
and on that farm he had some mice, E-I-E-I-O.

With a squeak-squeak here and a squeak-squeak there,
here a squeak, there a squeak, everywhere a squeak-squeak.
Old MacDonald had a farm, E-I-E-I-O.

Old MacDonald had a farm, E-I-E-I-O,
and on that farm he had a cat, E-I-E-I-O.

With a meow-meow here and a meow-meow there,
here a meow, there a meow, everywhere a meow-meow.
Old MacDonald had a farm, E-I-E-I-O.

Old MacDonald had a farm, E-I-E-I-O,
and on that farm he had some animals, E-I-E-I-O.

With a cluck, cheep, moo, and a neigh, oink, quack,
here a woof, there a baa, everywhere a squeak, meow!
Old MacDonald had a farm, E-I-E-I-O.